MNE

Presents

The Beard that Boosted Self Confidence

Kyle B. Hart

Old Fashion Publishing

The Beard that Boosted Self Confidence

Copyright © 2015 by Kyle B. Hart

Old Fashion Publishing
11251 SW Capitol Hwy
Portland, OR 97219

ISBN: 978-990678427
Printed in the United States
First Edition, Summer 2015

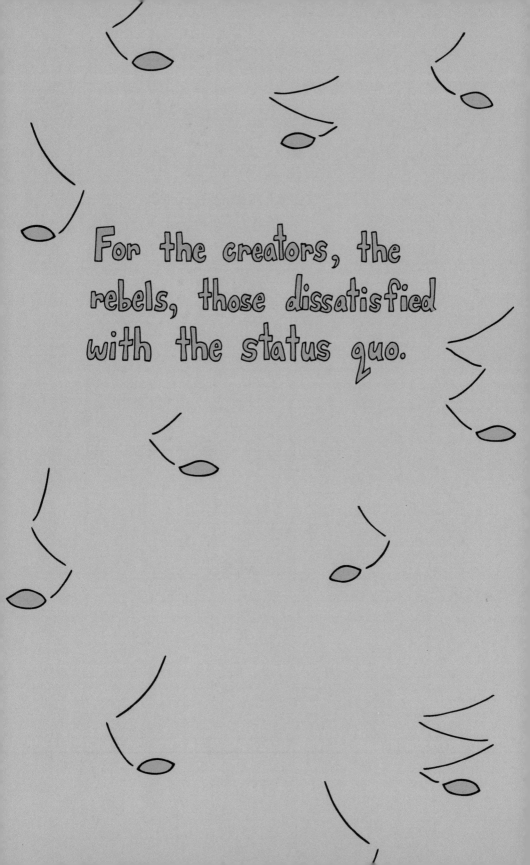

For the creators, the rebels, those dissatisfied with the status quo.

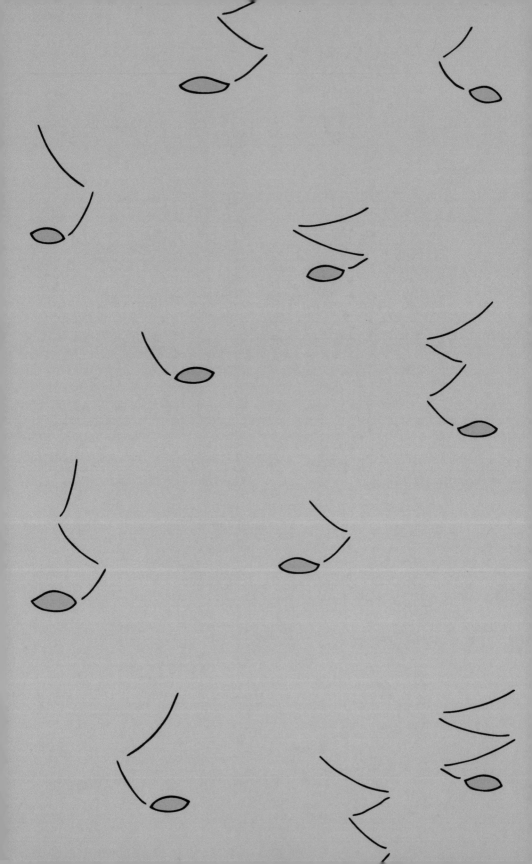

The temperature read 103 and Jerry's beard said, "I'm hot as can be!"

"I need a
cold river,
a stream,
or a lake!
It's too dang warm, for goodness sake!"

The actress on screen had lots of pride, succeeding in what she hoped for and tried.

to help

the world

outgrow its doubt.

The very first stop for this hero of hope

was a playground where

students were skipping

a rope.

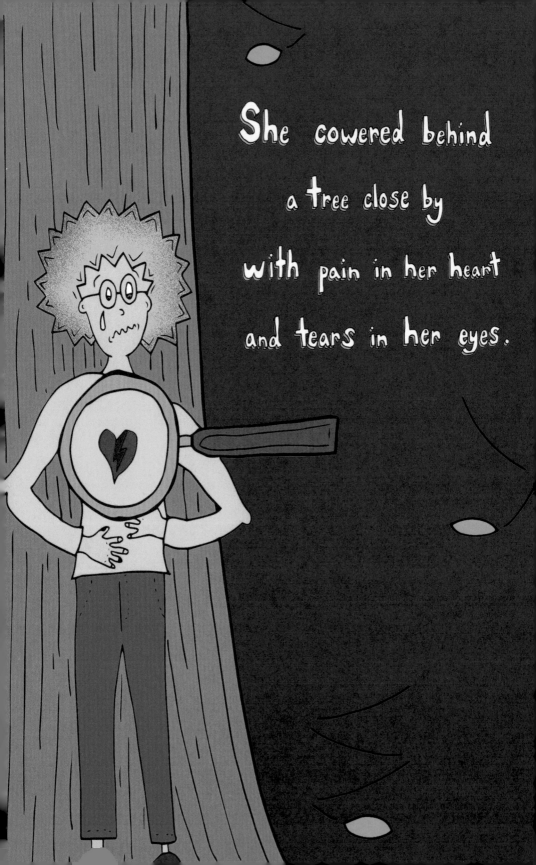

"I'm sorry those girls were mean and cruel,
but keep your chin up! You're super cool!"

Her nerves calmed down and fluttered away.

"Forget those meanies!"

yelled Nancy,

LET'S PLAY!

They pranced all recess in confident fashion
and made new friends named

Keaton and Ashton.

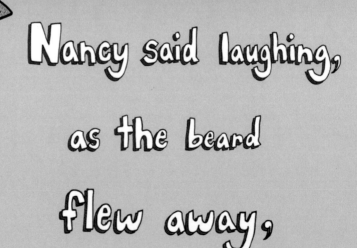

Nancy said laughing,
as the beard
flew away,

It zoomed down the alleys and
zipped 'round the blocks,
but stopped when it saw two
holey
brown
socks.

"But you can find some! Trust in your skills!

You can be happy

Bills

and pay all your bills."

He nodded and said,

"I'm bigger than fear.

With plenty of patience, I'll find my career."

"There must be a few clever tricks up my sleeve!
I've faced some rejection, but I still believe."

"Hey! What's the trouble? Why the glum face?"
"It's a girl," he said. "Her name's Anna Grace."

"I want to ask her out on a date,
but I'm nothing like all-star quarterback, Tate."

"Hey Anna,"
he said,
"Can I buy you
a smoothie?"

"Yes, please!"
said Anna,
"Then maybe
a movie?"

cried the beard,
not feeling
so great.

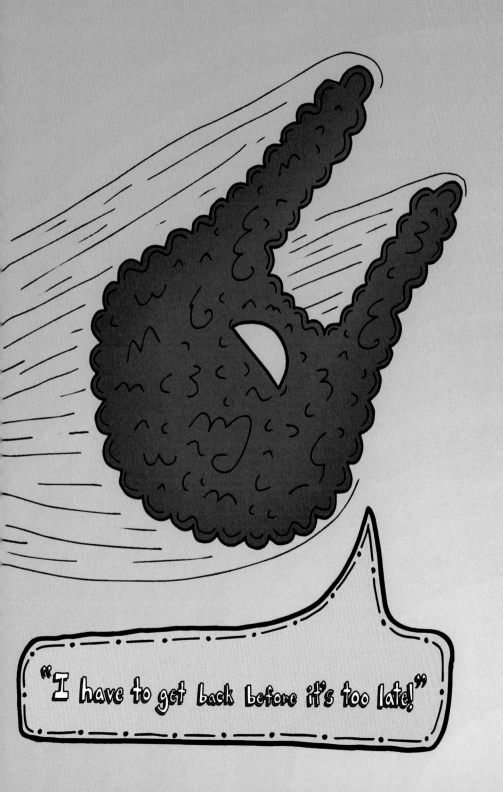

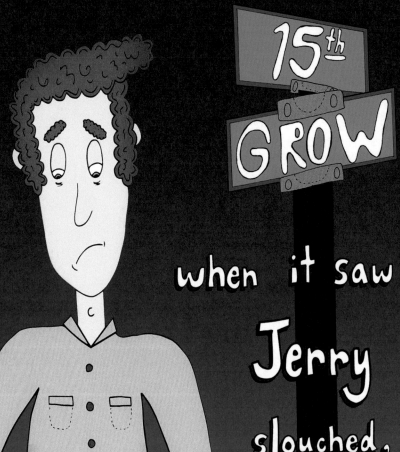

It rounded the corner of **15th** **GROW** when it saw **Jerry** slouched, his head hung low.

It smacked onto Jerry's no-longer-bald face and they both rejoiced in a scratchy embrace.

"It sure is amazing what one can achieve

when that person decides to simply

believe."

For the beard and Jerry,
the future looked bright

walking home
together
on a
warm
summer
night.

A special thanks to:

Derek Danielson

Daniel & Courtney Hauser

Dustin Hayes

Milk Flud

Ryan Harper

Zachary Cosby

Benjamin Ward

Alexander Crawford

Kate Adolphson

Tricia Morrison

Christopher Skelley

Mom & Dad

Jeffrey Hale

Courtney & Wayne Pierce

Made in the USA
Middletown, DE
23 March 2019